Quentin Blake

John Yeoman

BEATRICE AND VANESSA

ANDERSEN PRESS

This paperback first published in 2011 by Andersen Press Ltd.
Published in Australia by Random House Australia Pty.,
Level 3, 100 Pacific Highway, North Sydney, NSW 2060.
First published by Hamish Hamilton, 1974.
Text copyright © John Yeoman, 1974
Illustration copyright © Quentin Blake, 1974
The rights of John Yeoman and Quentin Blake to be identified as the
author and illustrator of this work have been asserted by them in
accordance with the Copyright, Designs and Patents Act, 1988.
All rights reserved.
Colour separated in Switzerland by Photolitho AG, Zürich.
Printed in China.
Quentin Blake has used pen and ink and watercolour in this book.

10   9   8   7   6   5   4   3   2   1

British Library Cataloguing in Publication Data available.
Trade ISBN 978 1 84939 269 3
Special Sales ISBN 978 1 78344 238 6

This book has been printed on acid-free paper

This is Beatrice.

This is Vanessa.

Beatrice, the ewe, and Vanessa, the nanny-goat, had spent their lives together in the same field. Every day for as long as they could remember they had nibbled the same grass, ambled slowly round the same farm buildings, rubbed their sides against the same tree, and stood nattering together with their chins resting on the same gate.

Today seemed specially dull. The grass was limp and tasteless, and neither of them could think of anything new to talk about.

"We should take a holiday," said Vanessa suddenly.

"Now?" asked Beatrice, who was much more timid than her friend.

"There's no time like the present," said Vanessa, "Let's pack straight away!"

"But you know we haven't anything to pack," said Beatrice.

It was true. But Vanessa had another idea.

"We'll borrow one or two things from the farmhouse," she said. "They had a party there last night, so nobody will be up yet."

Beatrice looked uncertain. "After all," said Vanessa, "we can always return the things when we come back."

As they walked off to the silent farmhouse to see what they could find, Beatrice was filled with admiration for her clever friend.

There was no one about in the farmhouse.

"Do you see anything you fancy?" asked Vanessa. Beatrice noticed a beautiful bunch of balloons which had been tied on to a stuffed wolf's head on the wall.

"They would make me feel on holiday," she said in an excited voice.

"There doesn't seem much else besides this old shopping bag on the table," said Vanessa. "I suppose we might as well borrow that and the wolf's head too."

Vanessa clambered onto the table and passed down the wolf's head for Beatrice to pop into the shopping bag. Then she freed the string of the balloons from around its neck so that Beatrice could take hold of it.

The two friends crossed the farmyard and squeezed through a hole in the hedge, being very careful not to get the balloons tangled up. Then they set off from the farm for the first time in their lives.

They travelled slowly because they ate grass all the time as they went along. It certainly tasted sweeter and fresher than the farmyard grass. Without noticing it, they nibbled their way into a dark forest.

And then suddenly, to their alarm, they looked up to find themselves face to face with a pack of lean, hungry wolves.

"Welcome ladies," said the leader of the wolves. "You are just in time for dinner. Isn't that so, boys?" And the whole pack of wolves started chuckling.

Beatrice was so frightened of them that she let go of her balloons, which went floating up and away into the forest. But she trusted her sensible friend to think of something.

"Thank you for your kind invitation, gentlemen," said Vanessa, "but I'm afraid we're on a diet at the moment. But we'd be delighted if you'd share our meal with us." She turned to Beatrice and whispered something in her ear. "My friend will just have a look to see if there is anything tasty in our bag," she said. As Beatrice, with shaking hooves, began to rummage in the bag, Vanessa added: "Not the fat one, of course. And certainly not the stale one."

Finally, Beatrice timidly lifted out the stuffed wolf's head.

"Wonderful," said Vanessa. "That's what I call a really fresh, juicy one. Have we six or seven more like that in there?"

Beatrice had no time to reply. There was an
ear-splitting howl as the terrified wolves
fled into the depths of the forest.

They ran and ran until at last they found their path
blocked by an enormous bear.

"What's the matter?" he asked.
"Is there a fire in the forest?"

All the wolves began explaining at once, but finally the
leader was able to tell the bear what had frightened them.
"A ewe and a nanny-goat, eh?" said the bear, licking his
lips at the thought. "Well, if they only eat wolves, I've got
nothing to worry about. Just lead me to them and I'll take
care of them for you."

"They can't have gone far," said the wolf leader.

So the whole
howling pack, followed
by the bear, turned round and raced back
through the forest. The fearful noise they made
sent all the little forest animals scampering
ahead of them in alarm.

Beatrice and Vanessa were puzzled to see a
number of squirrels streak past them.
"Up a tree, quickly," squealed the squirrels.
"The wolves are coming."

Although they didn't feel very happy about climbing trees, Beatrice and Vanessa saw that it was the only thing to do. "After all," said Vanessa, as she hoisted her nervous friend on to a low branch, "they'll never think of looking for us up a tree."

The fat bear, who was quite out of breath after his long run, collapsed panting at the foot of the very tree in which Beatrice and Vanessa were hiding. He wiped his forehead with his paw. "You chaps spread out and look for the ewe and the nanny-goat while I sit here and organise things," he said.

Beatrice was having great difficulty in keeping her balance on her thin branch above the bear's head.

"I'm afraid I can't hold on much longer," she whispered.

Vanessa noticed a piece of string dangling through the
leaves. She looked up and saw that Beatrice's balloons had
drifted into the next tree and were stuck in a branch just
above their heads.
"Don't panic, Beatrice," she said, reaching across and
pulling the balloons down very gently.
"Just do what I do."

When the balloons were
within reach, clever Vanessa
began stabbing at them with
her little hooves, making them explode:

BANG! BANG! BANG!

And they began shouting at the tops of their voices:

"There's a bear!"

"Set the dogs loose!"

"Don't let him get away!"

Without knowing what was happening, the
bear and the pack of wolves fled off again,
howling, into the forest.

Vanessa clambered to the ground and helped
Beatrice down. Then with the shopping bag
and the wolf's head, but without their
balloons, they made their way together out
of the forest.

Back at the farm they still nibble the same dry grass, rub their sides against the same tree, and carry on their never-ending conversation at the same gate.

But now they really have got something to talk about.

Also illustrated by Quentin Blake: